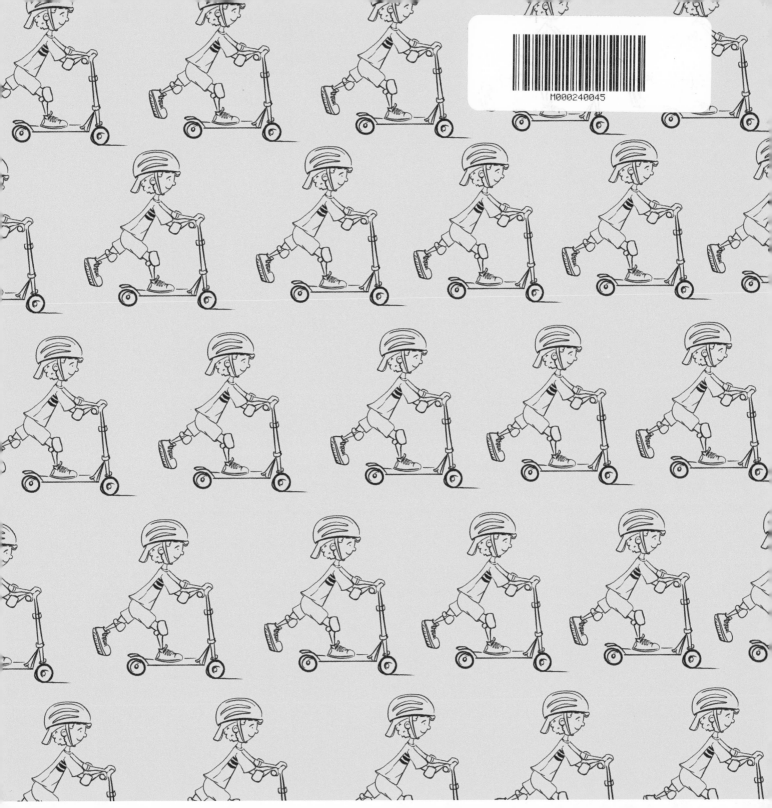

Dedicated to our Busy Bees

Noah, Gavin, Levi,

Julian, Adrian, and Cameron

Copyright © Amaka Chinegwu Alcocoer
Illustrations © Adia Guidry
All rights reserved.
Colorado Springs, CO
2021

Library of Congress Control Number: 2021903657
ISBN 978-1-7366100-0-8

Wait For It

By Amaka Chinegwu Alcocer

Illustrated by Adia Guidry

Some things take too long.

Like waiting for a pie to finish baking.

And waiting for the rain to stop.

And driving to Auntie's house.
And especially waiting for a special delivery.

That was Busy's current situation.

Busy wasn't his real name, but that's what his family called him

because he was always up to something and he didn't like waiting around.

His Granny called him on Monday to tell him that she was going to send him a package.

It was hard for Busy to practice patience, but he has learned from his parents that it's easier to wait for something if you stay distracted.

So on Tuesday, he built a grand castle with his building blocks to pass the time, but his package still didn't arrive.

On Wednesday, he read through all the books on his shelf, but his package still didn't arrive.

On Thursday, he made cakes, muffins, and pies, but his package still didn't arrive.

By Friday, he was feeling really anxious.

He painted pictures all day long. He was about to go inside when finally...

his package was delivered!

It was a new hat!

Some things take too long, but oftentimes they're worth the wait.

Meet the Author and the Illustrator

Amaka Alcocer & Adia Guidry

Sisters that believe in the magic of books who are on a mission to create more featuring black and brown characters.

CPSIA information can be obtained
at www.ICGtesting.com
Printed in the USA
LVHW071016090521
686912LV00001B/44